The Nutcracker.
Casse-Noisette
P. Tschaikovsky.

Preface

The Nutcracker *has become a permanent and beloved part of our Christmas celebrations. The ballet is danced to packed houses, and generations of ballet lovers have grown up and expanded the audience over the years. With a marvellous symmetry, so have dancers performed in* The Nutcracker *as children, annually moving up in the various roles, keeping the very tradition of ballet alive as several generations share the stage. I have danced the Snow Queen and Sugar Plum Fairy in* The Nutcracker *almost every year of my professional life, which has been twenty years long; and before that, I portrayed Clara at the age of nine.*

I believe it to be the music with its glorious score by Peter Ilyich Tschaikovsky that has immortalized The Nutcracker *and ensured its continuity. With the myriad productions mounted all over the world every holiday season, the music's inspired genius is the only constant amongst a seemingly infinite variety of versions. The music charms, and always one feels like dancing!*

The story of The Nutcracker *lives with the freshness of tradition because there will always be a desire and a need for fantasy. The original work by Hoffmann was dark and arresting, and not at all frivolous. I have tried to retell it in the style of Toller's paintings, romantic, exotic and with a faith in the existence of magic.*

THE NUTCRACKER

by E.T.A. Hoffmann

Retold by Veronica Tennant

Illustrated by Toller Cranston

McClelland and Stewart

The Canadian Publishers
McClelland and Stewart Limited
25 Hollinger Road, Toronto M4B 3G2

Canadian Cataloguing in Publication Data

Hoffmann, E. T. A. (Ernst Theodor Amadeus),
1776-1822.
    The Nutcracker

Translation of: Nussknacker und Mausekönig.
ISBN 0-7710-2316-2

1. Fairy tales. I. Tennant, Veronica.
II. Cranston, Toller. III. Title.

PZ8. H64Nu 1985   j833′.6   C85-099313-X

Music on endpapers by John Kerr

Printed and bound in Canada by D. W. Friesen

*To my mother, Doris, and my daughter, Jessica,
for whom* The Nutcracker *is always special.*
— *Veronica*

To the memory of Sir Edward Charles and Dr. Nijinsky.
— *Toller*

hristmas was coming. How Clara loved the first whispersoft snowfall. With it came plans and lists and those little glances exchanged between Mama and Papa. Clara's illustrious parents, Judge and Mrs. Silberhaus, would become like children in their eagerness to celebrate the season. And they shared their richness of spirit and fortune with a munificence unmatched in all of Nuremberg. Clara had long ago discovered that her home, with its vaulted arches and stained-glass windows, its inlaid floors and marble mantels, was much venerated in the city. But never did she feel so proud of its warm splendour as at Christmas.

As soon as December arrived, preparations would begin. First, there was the visit to the Kris Kringle market where, amid the heady confusion of Christmas colours and smells, the Silberhaus family would cram their shopping baskets with exotic spices, exquisite hand-carved ornaments, apricots, almonds and chocolates. Children and parents would then dart about, mysteriously clutching sealed packages. And at the end of the day they would collapse where they always did — at the stall with the hot cider and cinnamon sticks and scrumptious potato pancakes.

Next, Mama and Anya, the cook, would take command of the kitchen, and all the marinating and baking and roasting would begin. Clara would roll the gingerbread, make designs out of the marzipan and try to keep the fingers of her mischievous brother, Fritz, out of the tempting bowls. Delicious fragrances would waft up from the ground floor and fill the house as each room was redecorated and scrubbed and polished till it shone.

Yet the regular routine of the Silberhaus family was collapsing. Doorbells disrupted, hammers pounded and a constant thudding of feet sounded on the stairs to all four storeys of the house. By the week before Christmas everyone was breathless with anticipation and exhaustion.

Clara didn't see much of her parents as the days flew by. "I'll be with you in just a little while, my darling," her father would say as he hastily shut the parlour doors. But not before Clara had glimpsed the pyramids of boxes beside mountains of coloured paper and tangles of ribbons.

And just when it seemed they could never be ready in time, Christmas Eve arrived, inevitable, miraculous and transforming. From the candlelit windows carriages could be seen collecting in the circular drive. Footmen in festive livery descended quickly to assist the elegantly clad gentlemen in top hats and tails and ladies wrapped in fur-trimmed capes. Chatter and laughter rang out in the crisp air and the guests greeted each other effusively, for an invitation to the Silberhaus mansion at Christmas was highly prized. The children, with scrubbed faces, brushed hair and starched collars, stared shyly at each other.

"How magnificent the house looks tonight!" remarked one of the guests as the doors swung open.

"Each year it appears more beautiful than the last," commented a lady. "It's a Silberhaus tradition."

Clara waited in the reception hall, feeling glamorous. This year she was wearing a special dress, one her mother had worn when she was twelve. It flowed to the ground and was made of a delicate Swiss lace. Underneath, a skirt of red taffeta rustled as she walked. Mama had braided a scarlet ribbon into her hair and had even let her dab on a few drops of the floral scent that was Father's special gift to Mama every Christmas.

The parlour had been out of bounds to the children for the past two weeks. Clara knew that Papa had plans for the Christmas tree. He loved to surprise them, but this year he had been closeted in there even more than usual.

Expectation rose to fever pitch as the younger guests congregated with Clara and Fritz outside the panelled doors. They had heard the exclamations of the grown-ups when they entered the parlour. Of course there would be the holly-trimmed cornices and pine-scented hearth, the dishes of candied fruits and gaily wrapped gifts, but it was the tree that they all longed to see. A lull from inside signalled that the oak doors were about to slide open. Instantly the children hushed their chatter.

To savour the moment she had so keenly awaited, Clara screwed her eyes tightly shut as she ran in. And oh the brilliance when she opened them! The fir tree reached almost to the eleven-foot-high ceiling. Its branches were iridescent, laced and dripping with crystal prisms. They twinkled in the light of candles that nestled in their own shimmering silver cases. At the top, holding a jewelled lyre, hovered an angel crowned with a halo of spun glass.

So spellbinding was the sight that Clara felt her breath catch. The children too were speechless. Then gasps spilled over words in their delight. No one had ever seen so beautiful a Christmas tree! And in a spontaneous rush they encircled it, young and old. Judge Silberhaus was the first to sing, in his booming baritone voice, and he beamed when his family and friends joined hands and sang a hearty salute to Christmas and the promise of the New Year.

The golden sound that suddenly filled the room was softer than the chorus but enough to bring quiet once more. In the bay of one of the windows a man sat in front of an instrument that looked like a miniature piano. Clara rushed over and threw her arms around his neck.

12

"Godpapa Drosselmeyer!" she cried. "It's been so long since we've seen you, and Mama didn't know if you'd be back this year!"

"No one can guess, least of all myself, what I may do," chuckled the strange-looking man. He was small, with a monocle over one eye and hair so white and wiry it may well have been a wig. "My, you've grown into a young lady," he said, turning Clara in his arms. "Just what I've been waiting for." And he laughed that deep, mysterious laugh which had fascinated Clara for as long as she could remember.

Godfather Drosselmeyer was a clock-maker who travelled the world in search of treasures for his shop of antiquities. Clara had seen it only once, when she visited Zurich with her parents. The shop had been locked, with a sign: "Open by Chance." No matter where Godfather Drosselmeyer was, every Christmas Clara's family received his gift of a clock. And when he appeared, often unexpectedly, Herr Drosselmeyer would spend hours tinkering with the gongs, cuckoos and chimes that resounded throughout the house.

To Clara he had sent dolls from all over the world, special ones almost too precious to touch, with porcelain faces and exquisitely fashioned garments that caused Mama to whisk them away "for their own protection." Papa had cleared a bow-glass cabinet for them, and there they sat, all twelve of them — beautiful ambassadors from such faraway places as Persia, Russia, China and Spain.

15

"My present for you this year," said Herr Drosselmeyer, "is from Germany because you're at an age of change, a magic time. You—" He paused. He was listening to eight deep-toned chimes. Clara followed his gaze to the mantel where a panther of gleaming ebony reclined. His eyes were extra-ordinary, two clear green emeralds, and nestled in his carved paws was a crystal sphere which encased the face and workings of a clock.

"You're too generous," murmured Clara's mother. "Not only is your clock magnificent this year, but you've given us this as well!"

Clara turned to the instrument that her godfather had been playing. "What is it?" she asked.

"This," he said excitedly, "is the latest musical invention straight from Paris. It's called a céleste. Listen—" And he produced sounds so sweet that Clara imagined she had been transported to some other land. She felt like dancing. "Oh, Godpapa!" she cried, and hugged him at the fading of the last, delicate note. "I think you must be a wizard!"

He looked at her seriously and merely said, "Indeed?"

As gifts were opened and admired, what laughter and exclamations filled the house that night! Clara had asked for a jewellery box and hoped for a silk shawl, and she received not only those treasures but many other wonderful things. Godpapa Drosselmeyer's present was always saved for last. She peeled away the tissue, expecting to see another china-doll face. Instead, a craggy nose, bearded chin and bright eyes peered at her from inside the box. As she lifted out the wooden figure, Fritz blurted, "He's ugly!"

Drosselmeyer nodded. "Yes, he is somewhat misshapen, but then, have you not heard the saying, 'Beauty is in the eye of the beholder'?"

Clara examined the carved man in her hands. He was a soldier, or perhaps a count—or even a prince! Lavish gold braid trimmed his painted hat and epaulettes. His colours were bold, with a crimson-red jacket and royal-blue pants. Buckled at his hip was a sword.

"My," said Papa, "what a handsome Nutcracker! Never have I seen one like this! Wherever did you find it, Drosselmeyer?"

"It's my business to discover the unusual," replied Clara's godfather. With a gentle "Permit me," he took the figure from Clara and lifted the stiff tails of the Nutcracker's coat. The wooden man's mouth opened to reveal several glittering teeth.

Clara was enthralled. What an odd and amusing present. The Nutcracker was passed from guest to guest and each time his mouth was opened and shut, Clara fancied that the quaint wooden man was winking at her. She laughed at the curiousness of it all.

The Nutcracker was not just a toy. He performed in an admirable way. No filbert, hazelnut or almond could withstand the power of his neat little jaws. Clara's Christmas gift became the centre of attention. Fritz, with his new tin soldiers, was growing increasingly disruptive and Clara decided to retrieve her treasure.

Drosselmeyer, who had a long journey before him, was the first to call the evening to an end. As Clara thanked him again, he took her hands and said in almost a whisper, "Bon voyage."

"But it's you who are going so far!" she protested.

"Ah, yes," he answered. "How silly of me."

By the time the last of the guests had left, even Clara admitted to being ready for bed. She pleaded with her mother not to take the Nutcracker from her—"He's not breakable!"—but Mrs. Silberhaus insisted he go under the tree with all the other gifts. Yawning, Clara could hardly climb the stairs to her bedroom.

he was afraid of the dark and always tried to fall asleep as soon as she was tucked into bed. But tonight her mind would not rest. With each rapturous recollection of the evening's events, Clara found herself growing more and more alert. Creaks, rustles and squeaks kept sounding in the dark. She stopped to listen, but now there was only silence. What was that? Sitting bolt upright, she could see nothing past the blackness of her open door. Wide-eyed, she lay down again, straining to make out what she thought she had heard.

Music! Clara was sure of it now, but she told herself it must be the clocks which were beginning their midnight chimes. The gong of her parents' new timepiece on the mantel rang out and Clara was suddenly overcome with a wild longing to see the ebony panther again. She slipped out of bed and made her way along the hall to the staircase. As she stepped down, she felt her foot catch in the ruffle of her new nightdress. She realized she was falling. Music flooded her head. She grew dizzy....

Clara reached the bottom, feeling strangely exhilarated by her swift descent. She seemed to fly to the parlour, reaching it just before the twelfth chime. Was there one more — number thirteen? Or was it the music she had heard, coming from the céleste?

Clara tiptoed closer, then sprang back in horror. Mice! Huge mice were running across the keys and now the music only hissed at her. Shuddering, Clara rushed to the Christmas tree, its glint ghostly from the coals of the fire. My Prince of Nutcrackers, she thought. He's made of hard cedar, he can protect me. Perhaps the fierceness of his face will give me courage to chase away those nasty beasts.

As Clara rummaged through the open boxes at the base of the tree, she noticed a large pair of shiny leather boots. She blinked. There were legs in them! She looked up at a sword, gold buttons, a silvery-white beard and smiling teeth. Amazed, Clara beheld her full-grown Nutcracker eyeing her with the most benevolent expression.

"My dear Clara," he said in a voice she almost recognized, "take my hand — we must act with haste."

A horrible hissing swallowed his words. From the darkest corner of the room leapt an enormous crowned rat, with a huge, twisted head and tiny, red-rimmed eyes.

As the Nutcracker unsheathed his sword, Clara clung to him. A bold swoop of his sword cleared a space by the tree, overturning the box of Fritz's toy soldiers. From a flurry of royal blue and scarlet they reassembled, grew in size and stood in formation. The lines were drawn; a battle was on.

Clara cowered behind silver branches as the soldiers beat their drums in defiance of the mice brandishing sticks from the firewood.

"We are outnumbered," the Nutcracker muttered. "We'll never overcome this evil by force. We must devise a different strategy."

Clara screwed her eyes shut, wishing away the darkness and terror. Light! That's what was needed. Seizing a long stick of kindling, she set it in the coals, then darted back to the tree to ignite its tapers. Strange, as she began at the lower branches, they would rise when lit. New branches would stretch before her, then climb upwards. The tree's incredible ascent was as deliberate as it was astonishing.

"Look!" Clara cried, turning around to show the Nutcracker. The room was now glowing with light. Emerald-green eyes the size of saucers stared out at her from the ebony panther which had grown enormous. The drums beat triumphantly. Mice, blind with panic, were scurrying in every direction. At the tip of his sword Clara's protector held a paralyzed Rat King, his gaze frozen by the giant cat with the eerie green eyes.

"Well done, my clever friend," said the Nutcracker. "Obviously these creatures didn't like your brightening their night world."

"But how…Why?…" Amazed, Clara pointed at the Christmas tree which even now was continuing to rise higher and higher.

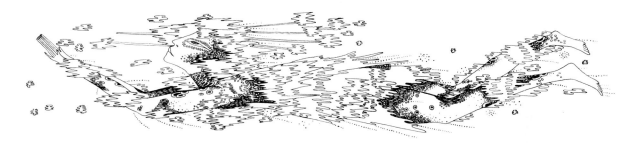

"Shhh!" A finger was laid across her lips. "Thanks to you, the spell of darkness is broken and for a few hours I'm no longer imprisoned in wood. Ask no more. Come—"

Clara clasped the Nutcracker's hand and indeed it was warm and firm. Music had replaced the strains of war, notes as pure as water, collected in waves of rushing beauty. And a feeling of overwhelming joy filled Clara's heart.

"Come, Clara," her prince spoke, "I will take you on a journey to the Land of Fantasy."

With these words the Nutcracker waved open the French windows of the parlour and lifted Clara into an exquisite sleigh with attendant reindeer. Soon they were soaring upwards into the stars. Snowflakes kissed her cheeks and caught in her lashes so that everything she saw seemed to sparkle.

"We'll travel through the Land of Snow until we reach the Ice Palace," explained the Nutcracker. He had bundled her in soft blankets and furs. Fast on his words, two glacial gates became visible through the mist. They opened to receive the sleigh on a snowy route that descended in a dizzying spiral.

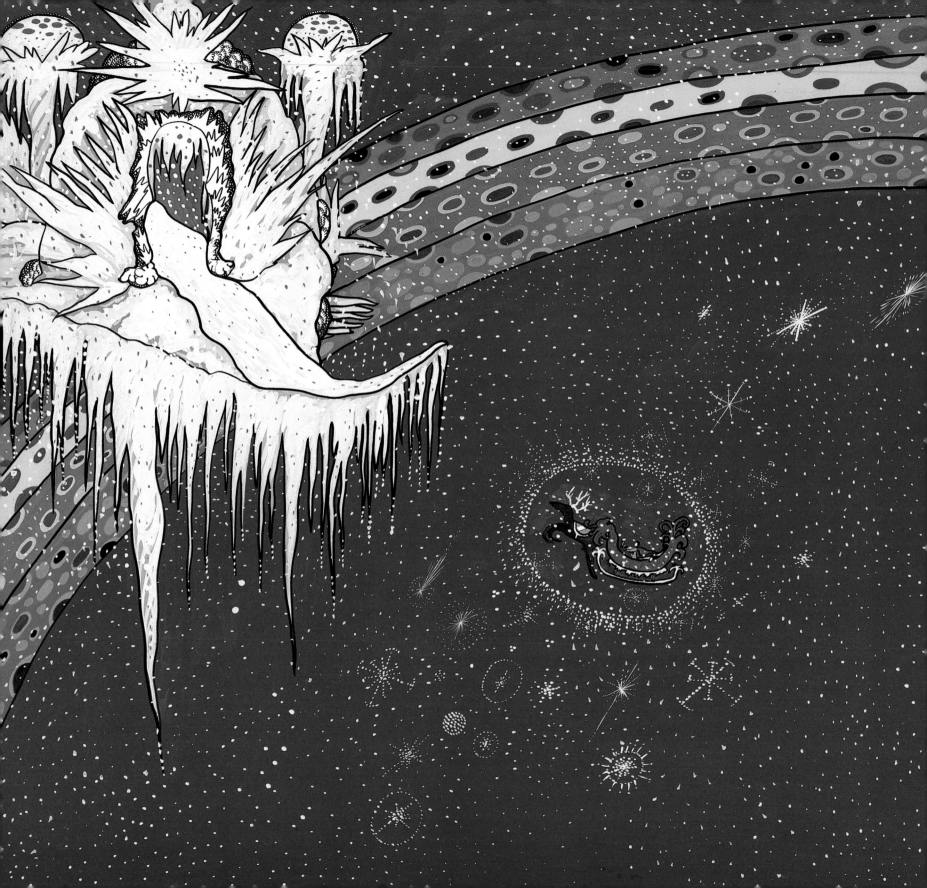

They had reached the side of a mountain, but on looking closer Clara could see a palace of intricate architecture carved in the snow. Icicles formed a portico over a sheet of ice in the shape of a heart. Before her eyes, it split with a deafening crack. Proudly, the reindeer drew Clara and the Nutcracker Prince into the palace of the Queen of Ice.

A chorus of angelic, silver-toned voices heralded their entry as they skimmed down a long hall lit with warming tapers. "We'll sup here, but remember to save room for our next stop at the Land of the Sweets," the Nutcracker whispered to his companion.

Clara and her prince approached a diamond-studded throne. There sat a woman of cool beauty. Her skin was pure white, with the translucence of porcelain. On her head rested a crown set with brilliants that danced and dazzled as they caught the light. The lady did not speak. She waved graceful boughs from which pear-shaped crystals hung in sweeping arcs. And with this signal, the choir sang out.

The honoured guests dined on dishes of sparkling crystal and sipped nectar from ice-filled goblets. Clara's appetite had been whetted by the evening's wonders and she savoured meats and breads that had mysterious tastes unlike anything she had ever eaten. The feast was served by jolly snowmen while beautiful snowmaidens dressed in white filigree wafted to the music and the graceful motions of the Queen.

Too soon the Nutcracker Prince was saying with some urgency, "Come, we must continue," and he guided Clara to the waiting sleigh. Craning her neck back as he swept her off, she could just see the jagged heart mend itself without leaving a trace of ever being broken.

As they sped through the mist, music rang in Clara's ears. It was clearly describing their journey and an expectant surge signalled they would soon reach their destination. The breeze caressing Clara's cheeks grew warmer, and the pale moon turned the colour of caramel.

"You are blessed, my young friend," the prince said to Clara, "for you're approaching the Land of the Sweets." He laughed with joy. "It's the place every child dreams of."

Clara smiled trustingly at her unusual friend—who seemed to be enjoying this wondrous journey as much as she. Somehow, she felt as if she had always known him. A question rose to her lips just as the Nutcracker pointed excitedly and the gates of another kingdom came into sight.

"Welcome! Salutations! Greetings!" were the sweet words that met the travellers as the reindeer slowed their paces to a contented halt. Blinking, Clara smiled back at the dulcet eyes and sugared lips of the gingerbread sentries encircling them. They rocked in a friendly, waggling dance to music that echoed their message. It was summery warm. The Nutcracker Prince shed all traces of his woodenness as he swung Clara high over his head and down from the sleigh.

What child can resist the melting of butter creams, the crunch of nut brittle, the taste of chocolate toffee? For Clara, whose sweet tooth had crumbled countless resolutions, the sight before her made her gasp.

She stood on a path stretched white, pebbled with mints, smooth and round. Lining the route were "croquenbush" mounds of little cakes encased in spun sugar—just like Anya, the cook, always made at birthdays! The surrounding meadows were filled with flowers: sweet peas, violets and buttercups. Before Clara's amazed eyes they waltzed, always in threes, creating beautifully intricate formations. Further on invited the open doors of a castle, its ramparts skilfully hewn from pink Bristol rock.

"At last! You've arrived! I've always hoped that someday you'd visit me in the Land of the Sweets!"

The words came from a vision of loveliness which had appeared on the front steps of the palace.

"Ah, my Sugar Plum Fairy," answered the Nutcracker Prince, "I too have dared to dream of this honour, but a spell had to be broken first—and for that we are forever indebted to my young friend Clara. Let me tell you with what courage she helped me defeat the Rat King of Darkness." And he described the midnight battle scene, making it sound even more horrible and treacherous than Clara remembered, with her own actions far more bold.

The exquisite lady then curtsied deeply and gracefully, her gown becoming a shimmering puff of pink. "Enter," she sang. "Let all the delights of my kingdom be yours."

Clara blushed at such homage but there was no time for reply as she was again lifted into the arms of her Prince. Whisked into the palace, down passages dotted with marzipan sculptures, she reached a magnificent banquet hall. There Clara was placed on a throne that smelled of cinnamon and cloves and was studded with multi-coloured sugar drops.

The celebration began with a light clap of the Sugar Plum Fairy's delicate hands. Instantly there knelt at Clara's feet a figure proffering a dish filled with turkish delights. Clara tasted the rose-coloured, mouth-watering sweets, hardly wondering how the beautiful Persian doll she had received two Christmases ago had come to this place. Almond eyes smiled secrets behind sequined veils, and Clara watched mesmerized as she wove among the court of spectators.

The click of castanets broke into Clara's reverie and she quickly looked up at the sly grin of her Nutcracker. He pointed to a Spanish dancer who now held centre stage. She too was familiar in her tiers of lace and satin, a red rose adorning her mantilla. Her dancing was passionate and lively. With a great flourish, she presented the guest of honour with a box of fan-shaped chocolates. Almost unnoticed, a Chinese maiden in pastel silk gently placed a warm tumbler in Clara's hands. Clara sipped the sweet tea, its steam carrying the fragrance of orange blossoms.

At a gesture from the Sugar Plum Fairy, Russian Cossacks bounded forward, bearing trays of crisp cakes drizzled with honey. To loud shouts and vibrant music, they gave an awesome display of leaps and spins. Her feet tapping, Clara feasted with sticky fingers. She giggled, for it hadn't escaped her that the Nutcracker was stealthily consuming as many goodies as she.

Then all thoughts of eating dissolved in the soft sounds that filled the air. At once Clara knew: such sweet tones could only come from a céleste! And they lent perfection as the lights dimmed and stillness descended, to the Dance of the Sugar Plum Fairy....

Her radiance, delicacy and generosity made her enchanting. Her satined feet skimmed the surface of the palace floor in loops and ever-changing directions, yet her arms drew flowing curves. There was a dazzling precision to her movements, but it was tenderness she expressed and understanding she gave. Like the pearls in her crown, the Sugar Plum Fairy shone with the quiet glow of perfection that runs deep in its simplicity.

A flawless jewel, her dance was complete far too soon for Clara, who could have watched forever! She could not contain herself when the fairy queen bowed modestly. Never in her life had Clara felt so elated. The music which had been pursuing her throughout the wondrous journey now surged and with its persuasive energy possessed her. She too must dance! She fell into the arms of her Prince, who deftly swept her about the ballroom. Tighter and tighter she gripped him as the pace quickened and the entire court—her Spanish, Chinese and Russian friends, the marzipan sculptures and flowers—whirled by in a delirious haze. She felt ecstatic, confused...dizzy...

"Clara...Clara!"

She clasped her partner more closely.

"Clara!"

He felt unyielding, cool, more wooden.

"Clara!"

She shivered, realizing that she was freezing in only her nightdress.

"My darling."

Clara blinked at the frowning, worried faces of her mother and father.

"You must let go of the Nutcracker," her mother said in a firm voice, "and let us examine your head. There's no telling how many hours you've been here. You've had a very nasty fall."

he days of fever were endless. Clara didn't count them, she didn't care. She had insisted that her Nutcracker be placed beside her on the pillow, and then her energy was spent. Listlessly she would hear the questions from the doctor who came to see her each day. But how could Clara answer? She was lost — lost in the music she could no longer hear. Sleep, dark and dreamless, kept her captive and gave her no rest.

And then one day Clara woke to the sound of a voice outside her door, a voice she realized she had been longing to hear.

"What's this, my dear!" Godfather Drosselmeyer boomed as he strode into the room. "They tell me you've been ill, fretting." He peered at her closely. "My, those flaming cheeks and sad eyes distress me." Taking her hand, he spoke more softly. "Dear child, forgive me for not coming sooner."

He sat with her awhile, saying nothing, and Clara sensed that her ever-strange godfather was waiting for something. His clasp tightened as the numerous clocks throughout the house proclaimed the midday hour. Absorbed, Drosselmeyer counted each chime, each cuckoo, each gong. At the twelfth stroke, a twinkle replaced the intensity in his eye. He appeared satisfied, even delighted, with the nearly synchronized harmony of his clocks.

Then, with ceremony, Drosselmeyer presented the package that he had been clumsily concealing beneath his coat. In spite of herself, Clara smiled thinly.

"Aha," he chuckled tenderly, "there's life in you yet! How I love to see the light return to your eyes."

But Clara was still too weak to struggle with the parcel's knots and ties, and so her mother unwrapped and lifted the gift out, exclaiming, "Dear Drosselmeyer, you've done it again!"

Clara ran her fingertips over the gleaming rosewood box that had been placed in her hands. Its surface was as smooth as satin. Imbedded beneath was intricate fruit-wood inlay and mother-of-pearl. In an ornately filigreed hole rested a key. Godfather Drosselmeyer took Clara's hand and together they turned it several times. They heard intriguing clicks.

Clara raised the lid.... At last!... Music! There was music again! Clara listened intently. Each phrase brought more of a smile to her lips and a sparkle to her eyes.

But the gasp came when Clara saw what the box contained. There on a pedestal was a miniature Sugar Plum Fairy, pearl-pink shimmer, pirouetting and dancing for her again.

"Oh dearest Godpapa, thank you, thank you!" cried Clara. "With this I can dream again! You've given me the key to fantasy forever."

Clara paused as a new thought crept into her mind. She sat up, radiant.

"And I promise you that I will share it."

"You must," whispered Drosselmeyer, his eyes glistening.

"Whatever can you be talking about?" Mrs. Silberhaus asked, as she checked her daughter's temperature.

Godfather Drosselmeyer rewound the music box.

"Just listen to the music, Mama," said Clara. "I'm going to tell you a wonderful story!"

Beside Clara, on her pillow, the Nutcracker smiled with his glittering teeth.

THE END